P9-DGG-068

Seven Little Postmen

BY MARGARET WISE BROWN
AND EDITH THACHER HURD

Pictures by
TIBOR GERGELY

A GOLDEN BOOK • NEW YORK
Golden Books Publishing Company, Inc.,
New York, New York 10106

A boy had a secret. It was a surprise.
He wanted to tell his grandmother.
So he sent his secret through the mail.
The story of that letter
Is the reason for this tale
Of the seven little postmen who carried the mail.

Because there was a secret in the letter
The boy sealed it with red sealing wax.
If anyone broke the seal
The secret would be out.

He slipped the letter into the mail box.

The first little postman
Took it from the box,
Put it in his bag,
And walked seventeen blocks
To a big Post Office
All built of rocks.

The letter with the secret
Was dumped on a table
With big and small letters
That all needed the label
Of the big Post Office.

Stamp stamp, clickety click,
The machinery ran with a quick sharp tick.
The letter with the secret is stamped at last
And the round black circle tells that it passed
Through the cancelling machine
    Click   whizz   fast!

Big letters
Small letters
Thin and tall—
The second little postman
Sorts them all.
The letters are sorted
From East to West
From North to South.

"And this letter
Had best go West,"
Said the second
Little postman,
Scratching his chest.
Into the pouch
Lock it tight
The secret letter
Must travel all night.

The third little postman in the big mail car
Comes to a crossroad where waiting are
A green, a yellow, and a purple car.
They all stop there. There is nothing to say.
The mail truck has the right of way!
"The mail must go through!"

Up and away through sleet and hail
This airplane carries the fastest mail.
The pilot flies through whirling snow
As far and as fast as the plane can go.

The mail is landed for the evening train.
Now hang the pouch on the big hook crane!
The engine speeds up the shining rails
And the fourth little postman
Grabs the mail with a giant hook.

The train roars on
With a puff and a snort
And the fourth little postman
Begins to sort.

The train carries the letter
Through gloom of night
In a mail car filled with electric light

To a country postman
By a country road
Where the fifth little postman
Is waiting for his load.

The mail clerk
Heaves the mail pouch
With all his might
To the fifth little postman
Who grabs it tight.

Then off he goes
Along the lane
And over the hill
Until
He comes to a little town
That is very small—
So very small
The Post Office there
Is hardly one at all.

HARDWARE

U.S.
POST OFFICE

The sixth little postman
In great big boots
Sorts the letters
For their various routes—
Some down the river,
Some over the hill.

But the secret letter
Goes farther still.

The seventh little postman on R.F.D.
Carries letters and papers, chickens and fruit
To the people who live along his route.

There were parts
For a tractor

And a wig for an actor

And a funny post card
For a little boy
Playing in his own backyard.

There was something for Sally
And something for Sam

And something for Mrs. Potter
Who was busy making jam.

There were dozens of chickens
For Mrs. Pickens

And a dress for a party
For Mrs. McCarty.

At the last house along the way sat the
grandmother of the boy who had sent the letter
with the secret in it. She had been wishing all day
he would come to visit. For she lived all alone in a
tiny house and sometimes felt quite lonely.

The postman blew his whistle and gave her
the letter with the red sealing wax on it—the
secret letter!

"Sakes alive! What is it about?"
Sakes alive! The secret is out!
What does it say?

DEAREST GRANNY:
I AM WRITING TO SAY

SEVEN LITTLE POSTMEN

Seven Little Postmen carried the mail
Through Rain and Snow and Wind and Hail
Through Snow and Rain and Gloom of Night

Seven Little Postmen
Out of sight.
Over Land and Sea
Through Air and Light
Through Snow and Rain
And Gloom of Night—
Put a stamp on your letter
And seal it tight.